EVERLASTINGLY

MICHELLE M. PILLOW

MICHELLE M. PILLOW® - MICHELLEPILLOW.COM

November 22, 2016 - #71 USA TODAY

Part of an Anthology

EVERLASTINGLY

*How do you find something
that you don't know is lost?*

ABOUT EVERLASTINGLY

On the run from her attackers and battered by a winter storm, Maura O'Brian battles her way through the snow, desperate and alone. She stumbles upon what she believes to be a secluded, abandoned farmhouse where strange voices are be more frightful than what awaits outside. The signs keep pointing to the same person—Jack. His very name fills her heart with such intense longing she'll do anything to find him.

Is Jack real or simply her fevered imagination hoping for a holiday miracle?

The Playful Prince
The Bound Prince
The Rogue Prince
The Pirate Prince

Captured by a Dragon-Shifter Series
Determined Prince
Rebellious Prince
Stranded with the Cajun
Hunted by the Dragon
Mischievous Prince
Headstrong Prince

Space Lords Series
His Frost Maiden
His Fire Maiden
His Metal Maiden
His Earth Maiden
His Woodland Maiden

Dynasty Lors Series

Seduction of the Phoenix
Temptation of the Butterfly

To learn more about the Qurilixen World series of
books and to stay up to date on the latest book list
visit www.MichellePillow.com

Snow was pretty until you were forced to run through drifts of it in heels and pantyhose. Maura couldn't feel the frozen blocks of her feet, but she forced them to keep going. Wet purple satin offered little protection. When she'd put on the gown that night she'd never dreamed the sleeveless decision would become one of the worst of her life. The party dress was meant to be fun and festive, not protect her from the elements. Though the knee-length skirt allowed her legs to move under a bulk of satin, gossamer and ribbons, it offered too little in the way of protection.

The trail she set through the untouched white was easy to follow, but there was no escaping it. For this reason she had to push onward. If she stopped, they'd find her. If she stopped, she'd freeze to death.

"Keep moving, keep moving," her brain repeated, an endless mantra pushing her legs on.

A whimper passed over her lips in a puff. This couldn't be happening. Not this. Not her. Not this.

Maura begged an unseen force in the universe to let her wake up, to make this a dream. She yearned for her parents, the police, a park ranger—anyone who could get her out of the cold. At first she'd just ran, as hard and fast as she could. The full moon revealed the bleakness of the Kansas landscape, the flat snowy field only broken up by lines of trees planted during the Great Depression to act like a wind block that would stop another dust bowl from choking the land.

Her father had told her that. It's why so many fields were lined with trees. These types of fields meant farmers. That meant farmhouses. Help.

She trudged on in mindless purpose. Deliverance from her icy hell came by way of a tiny light in the distance. She aimed for it, glancing back to see if she was being followed. Her eyes were so cold she couldn't be sure if they were figures in the darkness or protrusions in the landscape.

The light gave her hope and she pushed as hard as she could, running on adrenaline and fear. Soon the shape of a single window formed in the night, then the moonlit outline of an old house. Maura stumbled and fell against a wooden fence outlining the property. It took everything she had to lift her foot and launch her body over. She fell to the frozen earth and looked toward salvation. The front door creaked open bringing with it a streak of blinking interior light.

"Help," she whispered, trying to crawl before collapsing to the ground.

THE BLARE of a trumpet greeted Maura as she opened her eyes. Gasping, she flounced around on a musty bed, fighting before she could properly see that no one was attacking her. She took a deep breath and then another, waiting for her heart to stop pounding. A lantern cast light over the dusty room. Wallpaper curled along the bottom edge of the wall, exposing the old lath and plaster beneath. Tarnished mirrors and tattered curtains decorated the room, as if they had been forgotten and left to rot. An old skeleton key hung on a nail by a faded green ribbon, though there didn't appear to be any locks for it to fit into.

Fat snowflakes flurried past the window, lit only by the lantern light. Pulling the covers off her body, Maura noted her strapless purple gown had dried. Her pantyhose had been snagged and her shoes were missing. A radiant heater warmed the thick wood planks of the floor. She crossed to the glass pane, unable to see past the heavy snowfall into the dark beyond.

The people in the farmhouse must have brought her inside. Was she safe here? It was warm and she was alive. They'd put her into a bed. For now that would have to do.

Maura stumbled away from the window, feeling out of sorts. Her tarnished reflection stared back from the mirror. Brunette locks framed her face in a mess of large curls. The paleness of her skin reminded her of how close to death she had come outside in the elements. Redness rimmed her brown eyes, and she remembered the bitter cold against her face. Undoubtedly she'd be sick later and she was a little surprised a fever hadn't already set in. Though, now that she thought about it, she did feel strange. A dull ache settled over her, not necessarily painful, just a constant awareness.

She went for the door, but realized there wasn't one. Panicking, she ran to the wall and smoothed her hands over the old paper. She pushed at the diamond patterns to feel underneath. She lifted the mirror away from the wall, bumped her hip against the radiant heater, and pushed on the nail holding the skeleton key. There had been a way in, so there had to be a way out.

The window! She could crawl out the window. But go where? Out to where her attackers waited? Barefoot into the snow to die of hypothermia? Or stay inside where she was trapped, but at least warm. Someone let her in, saved her, they would surely check on her soon. They wouldn't leave her here to die. The solution was probably so amazingly simple and she was too tired from her ordeal to figure it out.

Maura crawled back onto the bed and pulled the covers over her body. It might smell musty, but it was warm and safe. All she had to do was wait.

2

No one came.

It was possible minutes felt like hours, and hours felt like days. Maura had no sense of the time, only that night and snow persisted outside. A woman could only wait so long before fear tickled the back of her thoughts. She'd pounded on the walls, stomped on the floor, tried to pull open the sealed window, stared into the tarnished mirror until her own face seemed to mock her. Then it occurred to her that she might be in an attic room and the door might be in the floor.

She took the lantern and placed it on the wood planks. Crawling on her hands and knees, she looked for a hinge. After exploring the length of the floor, pressing and pulling each and every board, she finally caught a glimpse of hope. A small door, barely large enough to crawl through, was hidden partially by the bed post. The tiny handle looked as if it had been built for a doll, but the tarnished brass keyhole was large enough to fit the skeleton key on the wall. Someone had carved, "Everlastingly," on the wood.

Maura pushed the bed aside and grabbed the key. The lock did not easily turn and she had to use both hands to find the strength to unlatch it. The small door swung open. A cool breeze whipped in to the heated room from the darkness beyond. She pushed to her feet and fetched the lantern. As her eyes fell back on the door, a light had turned on inside, and she didn't need the lantern to see.

A voice whispered from within, light and high like an excited child's, "Do you think she'll come this time, or run?"

"I don't know," another calmer voice answered.

"She doesn't have much time. She can't keep doing this. The house will not stand forever. Maybe I should go in and lead her from the door. I'm sure I can find what Jack wants."

"Quiet or she will hear you. Interfering does not help. We tried that."

"Jack?" Maura whispered, her body instantly

awakened by the name. Now was not the time for desire, and yet that is what she felt. Tingling erupted on her skin, a reminder of warm hands and deep kisses. But she didn't know anyone named Jack. How could she be aroused by a name? How could she feel safe and warm when she was trapped in an old house during a snowstorm?

With only one way out she reached into the opening.

"Someone should tell Jack she's escaping," the child decided. "I'll go. You watch."

NOTHING.

It was possible minutes felt like hours, and hours felt like days. Maura had no sense of the time, only that night and snow persisted outside. How did she get in this doorless room? Why was there no way out?

Frantic, she had torn up the withering prison, pulling curtains from the window, ripping the mirror from the wall, tossing the stupid key decoration to the floor. How could she be in a room with no way out?

What if her kidnappers found her? What if they

kept her here and had some kind of torture chamber in the basement? Snow or not, she couldn't stay. She had to run, to fight to survive. She vaguely remembered seeing an old farm truck outside before she passed out. If she pressed her face to the glass she could see the outline of it below. She might not comprehend fully what was happening, but there was a sense of urgency building inside her. She had to get help.

Grabbing the mirror, she threw it at the window. Glass shattered. She took the coverlet from the bed and wrapped the corner around her fist to strike the remaining glass pieces from the sill. She then swung the thick material around her shoulders for warmth, and to protect herself from the broken shards. Outside the window was a trellis of dead ivy, conveniently placed, acting like a ladder, and helping her climb down. She tried to carry the lantern with her, but it fell to the snowy ground and extinguished. Now, helped only by moonlight, she shakily made her way down the side of the house. She hopped off, away from the broken glass in the snow.

The cold stung her feet through the pantyhose as she ran toward the old pickup. The faded red font on the side of the blue vehicle read, "Jack Everla". The vehicle was from the early 1950s, with a flat solid windshield, headlights set into the grill, and a rounded frame. It was the exact model she'd wanted as a kid.

Maura yanked the creaky metal door open before crawling inside. There were keys in the ignition but the dead engine did not so much as whimper with life. She was so cold already and didn't want to run again. There might not be another house for miles. Considering her options, the farmhouse seemed like the safest bet. She had no proof the people inside were dangerous. They might be upset that she broke their window, but she could offer to pay for it.

With little by way of a choice, she made her way to the rickety porch. The dark windows revealed only shadowy hints of what was inside. She pressed her face to the glass, trying to see. It didn't take long before she tried the door. As she pulled it open, light cut the dark porch. The glow from a Christmas tree lit the front room, the tiny white bulbs blinking slowly. She had not been able to see it through the outside window, which made no logical sense. Like the doorless room above, the home was covered in dust.

Maura remained quiet. Her bare feet made tracks on the floor as she closed herself in. Pictures hung on the wall and she smudged her fingertips through the dust on one to reveal dark eyes in a handsome face. The man was not smiling, as appeared to be customary in old sepia photographs. A thin scar ran over his left temple. Something about him looked familiar, creating feelings of warmth, but he'd probably died years ago. Still, she found herself standing for a long time, staring at his face, trying to remember why he might look familiar. Perhaps she knew his grandson? Dated his grandson? She swiped her finger over his chin to reveal his mouth. Her lips prickled with awareness, like she had kissed that mouth before and wanted to do it again —desperately.

"Are you Jack Everla?" she whispered. The name Jack sounded familiar, as if she'd said it a hundred times, but that made no logical sense. Nothing here made sense.

The soft sound of a record caught her attention and pulled her away from the handsome picture. She tiptoed toward it. The coverlet dropped from her shoulders. Brass and woodwind instruments played Big Band music, the crisp sound punctuated by the occasional bump and scratch of a record needle. Such music was meant to be loud, not soft.

Wooden stairs creaked as she made her way up

them, no matter that she tried to tiptoe. A faint light came from beneath a door, drawing her toward it. The music became louder. She turned the oval nob and stepped inside the room to confront whoever was there. The second she was through the door, the music abruptly stopped as if it had never been.

The doorless room.

The broken window had been repaired and the area tidied as if she'd never been there. She turned to leave but the door had disappeared and she slammed into the wall in her haste.

"Ow!" Maura gasped, putting her hand over her injured nose.

"We should tell Jack she's lost," a child's voice said. "It never takes this long."

"I opened the door for her," another young voice answered.

"You should not have done that. The others will be mad if they find out you interfered."

"What else could I do? Jack wants her to come. It's been too hard for her to find it this time."

Shaking, Maura looked around to see who was talking. Instead, she found something she had not seen before—a small door in the wall just big enough to crawl through. A skeleton key had been fitted in the lock. Though she listened, the voices did not come back. What choice did she have? She couldn't stay locked up. The old truck didn't run. The farmhouse was abandoned. Those were the first voices she'd heard since her run through the snow. It took a long time before she found the nerve to go toward the opening.

No way out.

How did she get in this doorless room? Where was the person who pulled her from the snow? She didn't remember coming up here, so someone had to bring her. Why didn't they let her out of the room? Or at least check on her?

It was possible minutes felt like hours, and hours felt like days. Maura had no sense of the time, only that night and snow persisted outside. She swiped at her eyes and paced the wood plank floor. The key had to mean something.

Where there was a key, there was a lock.

Holding the skeleton key, she looked for a hole to fit it in. She lifted the curling wallpaper, ran her hands over the floor. The radiant heat kept her from trying to go out the window. Her feet still stung from her run through the snow and there was no way she was facing those elements again. It would be better to find a way downstairs. Maybe they would have a phone. Or boots and a coat. Or truck keys. She vaguely remembered seeing an old farm truck before passing out. If anything, the downstairs should be less dusty and there may be some food. She couldn't remember the last time she ate. Though, really, she didn't feel hungry so that wasn't an immediate priority.

If there was a way in to this room, there was a way out.

She knocked on the bed posts and found them to be solid. Throwing the side of the coverlet up, she searched under the mattress. Her hands hit an old book and she pulled it out. Butterfly stickers clung to the journal's cover. In very curvy writing that reminded Maura of being in middle school, a young girl had written, over and over, on the pages, "Mrs. Taylor, Mrs. Jack Taylor, Mr. and Mrs. Jack Taylor", along with doodles of man and a woman together doing various mundane things—driving a car, eating in a restaurant, watching television. Whoever the girl was, her pictures were much less graphic than Maura's would have been at that age.

Next, Maura looked under the bed and found a small door with a tiny knob. The word, "Everlastingly," had been carved on the wood. How strange that she hadn't noticed it before. She was sure she'd never seen anything quite like it. The keyhole was the perfect size for the key. She rushed to it and thrust it in the lock. She was crawling out of her skin. She had to get out of the room. Anywhere was better than here.

Opening the door, Maura was met with a gentle illumination. She thrust her head inside the opening to look. A wooden wall blocked her view, but she saw the light coming from around the corner.

"Sh," she thought she heard someone whisper.

"That was too fast," a second voice answered. "She couldn't have found anything useful."

"Maybe she'll turn around. Sometimes she turns around."

"Who's there?" Maura called as she reached her arms through the opening and pushed against the wall to pull her body through. "Are you the girl who wrote the journal? Is this your room?"

"Too soon, too soon," the voice said. "Warn Jack."

3

THE BULKY WEIGHT of Maura's satin skirt caused her hips to catch on the miniature doorframe. She pushed harder, heaving her body through the small opening. Looking up, she found the ceiling was too short to stand. Maura crawled toward the light coming around the corner. When she reached it and peeked around the side, she found the light had moved around another corner.

Much like a mouse in a maze, she scurried on her hands and knees, turning corner after corner, trying to catch the light. Her palms ached. The wooden planks of the floor were padded only by the material of her skirt under bruised knees. The deeper she went into the tunnel, the faster she moved, desperate to get out.

The air became colder, a slight breeze that smelled of the outdoors. The yellow glow of light morphed into the blue tint of moonlight. She crawled from the tunnel and out of a snow-covered mound of earth. A forest stretched around her. The dense overgrowth blocked all but tiny dancing spots of light.

"You made it." The male voice was punctuated by the slam of wood on wood.

Maura gasped and spun around in time to see a figure locking the tunnel shut so she couldn't go back. She backed away from him, dragging her bare feet in the snow. Forest litter poked her arch and she stumbled.

The man turned to her. He wore a dark cloak and breathed hard as if he'd run a long way. Dark eyes were familiar, but a fleeting familiar, a face in the crowd, a passenger on a bus. She couldn't place him. A thin scar formed over his left temple, the wound long healed.

"You are early." He smiled, a charming look meant to draw her in, but she didn't trust that smile.

"Who are you? What do you want? Why did you lock me in that room?" Maura lifted her hand to keep the stranger back. "Don't come near me!"

"My name is Jack. I—"

"Jack Taylor?" Was that his house? The child-hood home of his wife? The idea of him being married struck her hard and she found she didn't like it. Though, there was no logical reason as to why she should be jealous.

"Oh, so it was the journal this time." Jack seemed disappointed by the revelation.

"Were you watching me?" Maura eyed him cautiously. "Is this some kind of sick-o game?"

"Game," he repeated sadly. "Oh, how I wish."

Maura's breathing deepened.

"You're going to run, aren't y—"

Maura didn't wait for him to finish. She bolted from the now locked tunnel. Though snow blanketed the ground, it didn't feel as thick as her first run, nor was it as cold. Perhaps she had lost permanent feeling in her feet. She darted through the trees, torn between the easier path for speed and the thicker brush for stealth.

Slowly the snow cleared, as if she ran through the winter season, and she erupted from the dense trees into a valley. Warmth surrounded her—not the artificial warmth of radiant heat fighting back winter, but the sunlight warmth of spring. Tiny gasps greeted her as butterflies leapt into the air.

"Maura!" Jack yelled behind her.

The butterflies swooped forward in formation like tiny planes. She tried to dart past them, but they re-angled and blocked her escape.

"Maura, stop," Jack said, catching up to her.

For some reason she was compelled to obey. Fear filled her but it wasn't fear of him. In fact, she wanted to turn around and stay with him.

"What is going on?" she demanded, looking at the dark winter forest, and then the bright spring valley. "Where am I?"

"Go," Jack ordered the butterflies. They instantly broke formation and fluttered around the flowers as if nothing had happened.

"What did you give me?" She was too scared to move. "I'm hallucinating. None of this is real. It's some kind of fever induced dream."

"We did not expect you back so soon. You are on the wrong path again." He pushed back his cloak to reveal a white tunic shirt and tighter black leather pants with cross laces up the side. Who dressed like that? Shakespearian performers?

Maura stared a little too long at his hips and became momentarily distracted by strong thighs and a tapered waist. Under different circumstances... "None of this makes sense. I have to run. I don't know why, I just need to run."

Spring felt safe. She wanted to stay but an outside force told her to run.

"There is still time to start over," Jack said. "Close your eyes and remember. You can find the right path. You have to find it."

Maura found herself obeying as she closed her eyes.

"Go back to the beginning and do it again," he urged.

"I want to stay here with you. I don't want to go," she said, desperation filling her. And it was true. It was nice here in spring. The gentleness of his voice calmed her. The look of him drew her in and she wanted to touch him, be with him.

"I know, but you have to try again. Go back to the beginning. You remember it, don't you? Snowflakes on Christmas Eve. They're magical, aren't they? Tiny perfect ice kingdom—"

"Perfect ice kingdoms doomed to melt," Maura finished.

"I never understood that." He chuckled.

"I was a little drunk," she whispered. "I was talking nonsense."

She had been admiring the fat flakes falling against her coat, not paying attention as she tipsily weaved her way from the Christmas Eve party toward her car. A lawn gnome poked out from the snow. The shoveled sidewalk had cracks in the old slabs. Dread and fear filled her with such intensity. Gasping, she fought the memory and violently shook her head. "No!"

When she opened her eyes, Jack stood closer than before. His hand hovered by her cheek. He didn't touch her, but the expression in his eyes said he wanted to. The yearning inside him was palpable and raw. Firm lips pressed together a little too harshly. Eyes narrowed in concentration as if holding back tears. He said, "Go back. You'll find it."

"I don't know what I'm looking for." Part of her wanted to obey the strange request, even though it didn't make sense. Go where? To the tunnel? To the doorless room? The fear came back as she thought of running in the snow. She didn't want to go back into the snow. It was warm here. Safe. Danger lurked in the snow.

She wanted to stay here. Forever.

It didn't make sense.

Her body told her to run.

"Stay away from me," she ordered, fighting the confusion. Jack's mouth had been on the verge of kissing her. She felt the heat of his breath on her cheek. Desperation shone in his eye.

"Remember," he whispered. "Everlastingly."

4

Maura felt the pull of winter down to the deepest levels of her soul. The warmth felt so nice against her skin and yet she still had the urge to run into the dark forest. It wasn't something she wanted to do, but something she was compelled by outside forces to do.

"You look tired," Jack said. "Maybe close your eyes and rest."

Maura's lids became momentarily heavy. She was tired. How could she not be after all she'd been through? Swaying on her feet, she mumbled, "I think I have a fever. I'm seeing things. I can't concentrate. None of this is real."

The back of his hand touched her forehead lightly. "Maybe you're remembering."

"What am I supposed to remember?"

"I can't tell you," he said. "I tried once. It didn't end well. It has to be this way."

"But we just met. I don't know you." She swayed again. His fingers felt familiar against her skin. The caress stirred a deep longing inside of her and it became hard to concentrate.

"Sure you do." His lips brushed hers softly. "Everlastingly."

"Why do you keep saying that?" She didn't pull away from his kiss. Nothing about this night made sense, but at least his touch didn't feel treacherous. Being next to him was the safest she'd felt all night. "Who are you, Jack?"

Instead of answering, he kissed her again. Or perhaps that *was* his answer—a gentle kiss.

Maura didn't move, just let it happen. Exhaustion made her limbs heavy. Her feet stung, a cold contrast to his touch. His fingers slid over her cheek and neck to cup her face. She felt him shake violently.

"Maura, please, find it," he whispered against her mouth. "I don't know how much time there is left. I fear all we have are these stolen moments."

Her lips moved along his and she didn't want to think about anything else. She pressed against his warmth, sensing that he might let her go soon. Needing to feel something other than cold, she desperately held him tighter. The firm press of his body molded against her. His desire was evident in the lift of his arousal, in the fevered exploration of his hands.

When she touched him, her hands knew how he liked to be caressed. Maura did not know this man, she was sure of it, but her body responded as if it remembered the taste of his mouth and the lines of his chest. Her finger remembered the indent of his spine under his shirt.

She wished he would just tell her what was happening. He clearly knew the answer. What was she supposed to remember? Why the doorless room and tunnel? Why such a place between seasons existed? How could he be laying her down in a spring-filled valley next to the wintery forest?

The soft petals of the field cushioned her. Maura refused to open her eyes, scared if she did she'd be trapped barefoot in the snow again. If this was her dying hallucination, then she wanted to take it. She hooked her thumbs into his waistline and pushed. With a little of his help, she managed to free his erection. The rest of his clothing seemed to melt from his skin to reveal the hot flesh beneath.

Emotion poured out of him in tiny bursts, pulsating into her nerve endings as if his desire for her was a tangible thing to be passed between them. The sound of his moan begged her for more. When he pulled up her skirt to tenderly grab her ass, she didn't fight it. This is what she wanted, an end to the torturous ache in her skin, to the uncertainty of her mind. Nothing made sense in this world but Jack.

Jack pulled at the bodice of her gown to expose a breast. His lips left hers only to find hold over an aching nipple. He tugged at her hose and she heard them rip open. The eagerness of his desire was in that very action, as if he couldn't wait to undress her fully. Seconds later his hips borrowed between her thighs.

They made love on the valley floor, bodies entwined, gentle but desperate. There was no hesitation as he entered her and in that second she knew him, and the feelings he stirred within her were familiar. Though she wanted the moment to last forever—as she tried to filter the pleasure of his lovemaking from the tease of her memories—their climax built to such a pitch that they had no choice but to fall over the edge. He stiffened over her and his breath caught.

Maura gasped and finally opened her eyes. A

tear slid over her cheek. "Jack? It's you. I remember. Everlastingly." The cold came back with a fierceness, starting at her prickling feet. The pain of it would not be denied as the threat of death pulled her into its heartless arms.

"Listen to me, Maura. The magic is waning. You must break the loop or we lose—"

"Oh, no, I feel it. No, no, no, not yet. Jack, not yet. Just one more minute."

"Remember me," he whispered as his body faded from above hers. Tears stained his cheeks in his desperation. "Remember Jack. Everlas—"

5

MAURA PRESSED her face to the glass window of the doorless room, trying to see through the falling snow. Someone had dug into the large yard, clearing the white away so that mud poked through to spell out the words, "Remember Jack Everlas".

The words were facing her window, as if they had been left for her to find. But who was Jack Everlas and why was she to remember him?

If someone wrote that on the lawn and it was still visible in the snow storm, then they had to be nearby. Perhaps below in the house? The room was high off the ground so maybe this was an attic and she just wasn't finding the right latch to get out. Taking the skeleton key off the wall, she used it to scrape at the window sill. It had been painted shut and it took a little effort to break the seal.

When she managed to push it open wide enough to crawl out, she hooked her feet onto the lattice and tried to close it once more, so the heat would not escape. The lantern from within the room cast light onto the snow. She made her way down the side of the house and then jogged to the porch. Peeking in the window, she tried to see if anyone was home. The house was dark.

Maura tried the knob. The door was unlocked so she let herself in. "Hello?"

No answer came beyond the flickering glow of Christmas lights on an otherwise bare tree. It actually looked sad, alone and musty, a half-hearted attempt at decorating for the holidays.

"My name is Maura. You helped me. I know it's silly, but I couldn't find a way out of the attic room so I climbed down."

Still, no answer.

It didn't look as if anyone lived here. The furniture was old and had been undisturbed for decades. Maybe the tree lights were the only ones that worked. It would explain why they were on, but no others. Just to be sure, she tried the light switch.

Nothing happened. At least the house was warm. That was something.

Tracks formed a trail down the dusty hallway. Someone had been here recently. She followed them cautiously. Glancing, she saw a clean swipe in the dust on an old picture frame that revealed a handsome face. The eyes were kind. Perhaps the owner of the farm in his boyhood days? She lightly touched the scar on his temple, wondering where she had seen him before.

"I wish men like you still existed," she whispered. "The dating pool is a sad thing these day—" A strong sensation filled her and stopped her words. What was she forgetting? *Who* was she forgetting?

The tracks led upstairs, probably to where they'd carried her to the doorless room. Maybe the note in the snow was their way of letting her know they'd be back. If they went for help it was possible their tracks leading away were lost in the snow, unlike the deep grooves they'd carved for their message. The old pickup outside hardly looked like it would run.

Instead of going upstairs, she explored the main level of the home. Most of the rooms were empty except for a few odd pieces of abandoned furniture. The kitchen had antique tins in the cupboard that read "Jackrabbit Tobacco" and "Jack-o-Lantern Pie Filling". A newspaper clipping with yellowed tape that no longer stuck to anything lay on the floor. It was a picture of an abandoned car alongside the road with the headline, "Mysterious Disappearance of Two Locals". The fragile paper crumbled to dust when she tried to lift it up to read the article.

Long ago someone had pasted colorful butterflies, now dulled with dust, onto a small door. Maura peeked within, only to find old wooden steps leading to a cellar. She felt around on the wall and found an old push button light switch. The lights flickered when she turned them on.

"Hello?" she called. No one answered, not that she expected them to.

Maura did not like the general feel of basements on a good day. Telling herself she'd just take a quick look, she tested each step to make sure it would hold her weight. Old limestone block foundation leaned inward and hard dirt made for an uneven floor. Cobwebs hung in dirty strings, abandoned by their spider makers. The lights flickered violently, threatening to go out. She began to retreat, only to stop when she saw a small chest on the floor beneath the stairs. It was tucked away and easy to miss.

The closer Maura moved to retrieve the chest,

the faster the lights flickered. She grabbed it and darted for the stairs. The lights went out completely and she was left stumbling her way back to the kitchen. Finding a seat on the old couch near the blinking tree lights, she placed the chest on her knees and dusted it off. The word "Everlastingly" was carved on the top.

A howl sounded outside and she jumped, dropping the chest to look out of the window. She pressed her face to the glass. The snowfall had begun to fill in Jack's name.

"Remember Jack," she whispered. A lost thought nagged at her brain. Who was Jack?

Maura turned to the chest. Pictures had spilled onto the floor like hidden memories—her memories. A Christmas Eve party in the dress she now wore, smiling and raising a glass of champagne. What was a picture from earlier in the night doing in an old box in an abandoned house?

Her hands shook as she reached for it. Tinsel sprinkled her hair in the photo, and she was smiling. Something small had sunk down into her glass, but she couldn't make it out. Shaking, she kneeled to the floor. The images didn't make sense. They were out of order—her car keys in her hand, her coat sleeve with fat snowflakes, tracks in the snow, a blurry face, a cracked stone, a creepy yard gnome.

And then blood—red crimson staining the ground, a destroyed snow angel, a lost shoe.

These were her memories, but she couldn't put them into order or context. She grabbed the chest, tempted to shove them all back inside as if they didn't exist. A dull ache formed behind her eye. Tree lights blinked over her photo's smiling face, an image that seemed to say, "Begin here", and so she did.

6

"Maura, a toast," a man said, the distant voice echoing through her mind. "I met you a year ago when you quite literally fell into my arms and gave me third degree burns with your ridiculously large coffee. But even as my face blistered, I knew I couldn't go to the emergency room until I got your number."

Maura gave a small laugh. Her lips moved, as they had when that picture was taken, and she answered, "At most I stained your shirt." The picture changed, as if the camera panned down her purple satin dress. "I only gave you my number because you made me feel guilty."

Laughter sounded, the tipsy happiness of a

party. The ghostly echo seemed to come from within the farmhouse, from a room she couldn't see. She slowly pushed up from the floor and sat on the couch.

The man continued, "Would you be quiet. This is my proposal."

Maura made a weak noise. Proposal?

"I had a lot of clever things lined up to say to you," he had said, "a lot of reasons why you should say yes, why we're perfect, but the truth is, when I look at you I forget everything logical. So, Maura Caroline O'Brian, say you'll marry me and make me everlastingly yours."

"Yes, Jack, yes," Maura told the memory. Jack's blurry photographic face came into focus. She remembered his smile and how happy she was whenever he walked into a room. She remembered their first fight, first kiss, and first date. So many tiny moments that created a relationship. She remembered what it felt like to be held, how her nerves would jump with awareness when he touched her. Whenever he was gone overnight on a work trip, she longed for him terribly. The desire to hold him seemed to choke her even now. From that first moment, she'd known he was her forever.

The ring had been in the champagne glass, not

that she'd noticed the lovely square diamond at first. Their friends had surrounded them in love. It was the perfect night, the happiness so intense that she feared it couldn't last. She drank too much and Jack had to help her to the car because she stumbled on a broken piece of sidewalk and snagged her pantyhose on a lawn gnome's pitchfork. She'd always hated that creepy gnome.

Maura looked at the picture of the keys.

"Give me those," Jack had said, snatching the keys from her hand.

"I wish it would snow forever," Maura had yelled, spinning in drunken circles into the street. Flakes fell upon her coat as she danced.

"Come here," Jack said. "You're covered in snow."

"It's not snow. They're tiny perfect ice kingdoms doomed to melt!" At the time it had made perfect sense.

"You are perfectly crazy, my love," he'd answered.

She wanted to spend her life with Jack. So much lay ahead of them that her heart had practically burst with the anticipation of their lives together. Getting to the car was a blur, as was the long stretch of wet pavement on a dark road, and the many signs advertising a local Renaissance Faire.

"We should go to that," she'd said with a laugh. "I would love to see you in tight leather, my lord."

"As you wish, my lady," Jack had answered. "But only if you wear tight leather, too."

Maura had chuckled as she watched streetlights glint off her ring until they disappeared, and then night swallowed the old highway. She stared at Jack's face cast in the soft lights coming from the car's dashboard controls. Big band music blared from the car radio. He loved that kind of thing and was always trying to drag her to revivals and jazz clubs.

"Did you look inside the ring before you put it on to show it off to the girls?" he'd asked, rocking in the driver's seat.

Maura laughed and slipped it off her finger. She opened the glove box for a light to read the engraving aloud, "Everlastingly."

"Everlastingly yours," was how they said, "I love you". It was special because it was theirs, unused in the centuries before, a new love, their love.

"Aw," she said, smiling at the sweetness of it. "Right back at you, baby, forever and ever everlastingly yours."

The memory became real, pulling Maura into it. Jack slowed the car and pulled to the side of the road. He unbuckled his seat belt and turned a very alluring smile to her.

"What? Here?" Maura laughed, even as she felt her willingness.

"I have been wanting go get you out of that dress all night." He slid his seat back all the way and reclined it. "What do you say?"

Maura glanced around.

"No one drives down here," he assured her, his tone dripping with honeyed persuasion. Jack reached for his belt buckle and unzipped his pants. His cock sprang free and he stroked it.

"We should wait until we get home." The words were unconvincing as she unbuckled her seat belt.

He took his hand from his shaft and reached for her thigh to push up her skirt. "It'll be like our first date."

Maura dropped her head back and laughed. "I did not sleep with you on our first date."

"But I thought about you straddling me in this car the entire first date." Damn, he had a persuasive smile when he wanted her. It worked every time.

Maura reached for her shoe.

"Leave them on." He pulled her toward his lap.

"But I'm wearing hose." She slid closer to him on the seat.

"Just rip them open with your nail and push your panties aside." He again stroked his cock and teased, "You better hurry. It's started to get cold."

"Let me judge." Maura leaned over to kiss his erection and he jerked as her lips wrapped the tip. She started to pull away when he pushed the back of her head gently and thrust up a few times. The firm pressure automatically caused her to suck him.

"As much as I enjoy coming in your mouth, I really want your pussy." He let go of her hair. "I'll buy you new hose."

Maura chuckled and reached between her legs to rip the delicate material.

"Oh, yeah," he breathed eagerly. "Now straddle me."

Cars were never an ideal fit, but it still excited her. As she straddled him in that tight space, she let her sex dance over the tip of his shaft. His eyes focused on her breasts as he took her by the hips.

"I don't know, Jack," she whispered, playing with him. "What if someone comes to check on us?"

The idea excited him more and he moaned. "I'll tell them you were a bad girl and I had to pull the car over."

"You like it when I'm bad, don't you?" She pushed down on him, letting him fill her.

"Fuck," was all he managed as she moved on top of him.

The position didn't let them get as deep as she wanted, but the physical contact was enough to stir her body toward a climax. Pleasure racked through her, and Jack's orgasm joined hers. Outside the snowy night was so quiet and peaceful, as if trapping them inside the interior of their own private snow globe.

Maura was pulled from the pleasure of the memory and her consciousness was once again in the farmhouse. She felt a tear slip down her face as she looked up from the picture-induced recollection to the actual tree lights before her, not really seeing them. She touched her ring finger, trying to slide the jewelry back on, and at the same time not finding the ring on her hand. Memories combined with the present in a chaotic symphony of blurred images and sounds. Wallpaper curled along the seams, held down by dusty pictures. A horn honked. The Christmas lights blinked, morphing into headlights and then changing back again. Her body swayed violently though the couch didn't budge. She struck her head against an invisible barrier.

Blood trickled down her face from where she'd hit it.

"Jack?" Maura moaned, holding her head. Her body stung as she tried to push up. The tree lights disappeared, replaced by the bright flecks of snow falling in front of their headlights. They had just made love and had parted so they could finish the drive home. Jack made a weak noise. Blood streamed down his face, coming from his left temple.

Maura blinked heavily before struggling with her seat belt. Grabbing her coat from the seat, she'd pressed it to the side of his face to get the bleeding to stop. "Jack, baby, it's ok. It's ok. I'm here."

He moaned in response.

She heard voices outside the car, but couldn't make out what they were saying. "Help! In here, he's hurt. Please, we need help!"

"Robert, shut 'er up," someone yelled. The man had a country accent as if he'd come from Southern Oklahoma. Kansans didn't generally talk like that.

"What? No. We need help," Maura called out in confusion.

"Look for her purse," the man continued, as if she'd not made a sound, "then pop the trunk. Hurry before someone comes by."

Were they being robbed? Maura moved closer to

Jack and searched for some kind of weapon while holding the coat to his head to stop the bleeding.

"Ain't no one coming by this late at night," Robert answered. "If they do we'll put on the hazard lights and say we found them like this. They'll probably give us a reward or something for being good Samaritans. Besides, it's not like you can tell we rammed them. This tiny car can't dent the beast. That grill is meant to plow down anything in its way. Just like me."

The window smashed behind her and she screamed in fright. Jack blinked, startled and dazed. Someone reached in behind her.

"Don't touch us," she yelled. "Just leave us alone!"

"Here. Check her purse," Robert said, snatching it from the seat and tossing it behind him. He smiled at her with a mouth full of tobacco stained teeth.

"Fuck!" his partner yelled, his voice coming from behind Robert. "Bitch only has twenty bucks."

"Not only twenty bucks. Just lookie what we have here, Stan." Robert unlocked the door and threw it open. "A prom queen! All dressed up and ready for the after party."

Rough hands pulled Maura's hair, dragging her

out of the car and into the snow. Her arms flailed, not doing much damage as she fought to be free.

"I never did get to go to a prom," Stan said.

When her attacker let go, she tried to crawl away. This seemed to amuse the men greatly. She screamed when Stan grabbed her by the skirt and pulled. "Where do you think you're going, prom queen?"

"I'm not a prom queen. Please, we're just on our way home from a party. There's no reason to let this get out of hand. Just take my purse and go." Even as she tried to reason with them, she couldn't keep the shaking out of her voice or the fear off her face.

Robert kicked her stomach to shut her up. Maura rolled onto her back, clutching her abdomen. He kicked her a second time, striking her along the outside of her thigh. Tears rolled down her cheeks.

Boots crunched the ground near her head. Legs towered along either side of her face. "Grab that ring."

Robert yanked her hand, ripping her new engagement ring from her finger. She watched him from the ground as he licked the stone before putting it in his pocket. "You should have brought more cash tonight, sweetheart. Then I could have paid for a lot lizard like I planned. But, since you didn't, I guess you can just take the whore's place."

"Stay away from her," Jack yelled. He charged their attacker, leaping over her at Stan and knocking him to the ground. "Run, Maura!" Jack punched Stan in the jaw before Robert wrapped Jack's arms from behind to pin them to his sides. Jack drove his feet into the ground and forced his body to fall back. Robert was slammed into the car. Blood splattered the snow from Jack's head wound.

"Jack!" She didn't want to leave him. She looked for a weapon but didn't find one.

"Get help," Jack ordered. "Go, Maura!"

Maura obeyed, running as fast as she could over the hard pavement.

"Stop her," Robert commanded. "Run the bitch down!"

Maura screamed and changed course into the snowy field. The cold stung her feet. She heard Jack shouting to run faster. She didn't turn around. Fear told her they were right behind her and she didn't dare look to confirm it.

Someone had to find her. Someone had to help Jack.

She wasn't sure how far she'd ran, only that she couldn't stop, even as she crawled through snow drifts with the little protection that wet satin and pantyhose provided. A farmhouse had to be around here somewhere. Someone had to be working these fields.

Maura knew if she stopped moving their attackers might find her. She tried to keep parallel to the road. Whispered prayers came out of her in tiny puffs of air. She begged an unseen force in the universe to let her wake up, to make this a dream. She yearned for her parents, the police, a park ranger—anyone who could get her out of the cold. Tears froze before they could fall. She told herself that she just needed to make it past the next line of trees, then the next, the next...

Coming to a fence, she whimpered, barely able to launch her body over. Maura collapsed on the ground and tried to crawl. Nothing but a field of snow stretched before her. Her calf muscles seized from the low temperatures and she couldn't feel her feet. Somewhere along the way she'd lost her shoes and hadn't realized it. Pressure had built under her head wound, swelling her eye shut. Her stomach ached from where she'd been kicked.

She'd gone the wrong way.

Just a small break to catch her breath and then she'd start moving again.

Rolling onto her back, she looked up at the full moon. The pain in her limbs was replaced by numbness. Snowflakes fell down upon her face but she did not feel them land.

"Jack," she whispered. Every ounce of her soul she had left was sent back to him, willing him to know how much she loved him. She prayed for him to be safe. "Everlastingly."

Salvation never came.

7

"Jack!" Maura surged to her feet. She didn't understand fully what was happening, only that she needed to find Jack. Her tattered gown was stained with blood, the gossamer fabric ripped, the satin covered in water spots. It hadn't been like that before.

Maura limped toward the front door, determined to find him. What if he was on the side of the road waiting for her to come back? She pulled the handle, but it wouldn't open. Frantically, she jerked at it, kicking and screaming to be let out of the dirty house.

"Jack! Jack!"

Remembering the upstairs window, she made her way, trying to find the doorless room. Her bare feet stomped up the stairs. There was only one door. She jerked it open and ran inside. The room was a mess, as if someone tore it apart while she'd been gone. The mirror was broken into pieces on the floor. The bed had been overturned, revealing a small opened door in the wall.

Seeing the word, "Everlastingly," carved on it, just as it had been carved on her engagement ring, she knew Jack was somehow showing her the way. Light came from within and she shoved her way through the narrow opening. Maura crawled through the tunnel, not caring where it ended up so long as Jack was on the other side.

She burst from the side of a snowy mound into the forest. "Jack!"

Maura turned in circles. Where should she look first?

"You..." Jack whispered behind her. She whipped around to face him. "You look different."

"Jack, the men..." She rushed toward him and ran her hands over his face to find the scar over his temple. "What happened? How did you escape? How did you heal so fast?" She looked him over to prove to herself that he was unharmed. Eyeing the tunic shirt and leather pants, she couldn't help a small laugh. "Where did you get those clothes? Did someone from the Renaissance Faire find you? I don't understand."

"You remember me." He looked too scared to move.

"Of course I remember you, Jack. We're going to be married. You just asked me earlier tonight. I..." Maura frowned and grabbed hold of his tunic shirt. "Wh—what's going on? Why are you looking at me like that? You haven't changed your mind, have you? It hasn't even been a day. I... Jack?"

"You said my name."

"Yes. You're Jack Michael Taylor. On our first date you told me your middle name was Susanna just to make me feel sorry for you. It worked because you made me laugh and I let you do more than kiss me that night after you got me home."

"It is you, Maura, it is you." Jack grabbed her tight and his whole body trembled as if he choked back tears. His hand rubbed along her back. "You found your way back to me."

Maura let him hold her. "How did you get away from those men?"

His caress stopped but he didn't let her go. "I got lucky. We fought. One of them dropped a gun. I pointed it at them and they got in their truck and drove away. The car wouldn't start because they'd rammed the front end. It was only four degrees that night. I took your coat and went after you." Moisture dripped onto her shoulder and she knew he cried. "I had a broken rib so I couldn't move fast enough. I'm sorry, Maura, I was too late."

"Too late? Jack, I'm right here. We're going to be ok."

"Maura, I'm telling you, you died. You've been dead nearly thirty years now. You have been trapped in a loop, reliving that night. I found you in the snow, blue and frozen. I wanted to die, too. And then the man in a black suit came. He told me that he couldn't change the fact that you were cursed by your circumstance to haunt the Kansas fields, but he could build a house where you had fallen, a house full of your memories that would call you in and lead you to me. Since that night you've run the fields, but you find your way here, to me, eventually."

"I don't understand."

"You're a residual haunting."

"Very funny, Jack. Do I look like a ghost to you?" She started to laugh, but stopped. "How hard did you hit your head?"

"Just listen, Maura. This strange man took pity on me because of our pain. He told me I had to sacrifice my life to give him enough power to make it possible. So I did because it meant I had a chance to be with you again. But he didn't tell me the catch. I couldn't go into your house or your memories, and you didn't remember what happened. Most of the time, you didn't remember me, and if you did, it was brief. I've lived for those seconds when you found me. If I try to tell you I love you, or anything else important, you loop back into your residual self and start running again."

"You're serious." Maura pulled away from him. "I don't believe in ghosts."

"Regardless." He nodded meaningfully at her.

Maura felt strange, but a ghost? How was such a thing possible?

"At first, you came back more often," he continued. "Sometimes you wouldn't find the way immediately and would choose the wrong path, but you would just loop again and eventually you would come through the door. Sometimes it took days, or weeks. Once it took less than a day and we were not ready for you."

"We?"

"The butterflies. The best I can tell is that they're like fairies. I hear them talking but I don't see their faces."

"Talking butterflies and ghosts and the grim reaper wearing a black suit."

He ignored her skepticism. "Over the years I have been able to piece together that you were in a room with a small door, and that's how you found me. You recognized me more back at the beginning. Your house was clean and the clues visible, so it led you to me easily—there were pictures on the wall, newspaper clippings, and clues to who we were. But as the years wore on, the clues became hidden in dust, the power in the house faltered, the clues of my name and face started to fade. It became harder and harder for you to find your way back, and I'd wait months to see you. The butterflies warned me that once the magic was gone you would no longer see the house and would loop forever unless you found the truth."

"He's not lying," a tiny voice said. Maura gasped turning to a bright yellow insect fluttering beside her. "Look at your feet. You're standing in snow and you're not even cold."

Maura began to shiver at the reminder of the weather.

"Your mind is getting in the way," Jack said.

Maura forced her body to stop reacting and the feeling of cold again went away. "I'm really dead.

I'm a ghost. So, any second now I'm going to loop and relive that night again?" The cruelty of such an existence was not lost on her. She wanted to cry, but at the same time she wanted to hold Jack and take every second she could with him. "Kiss me."

Jack pulled her into his arms and held her close. Their lips met. She moaned into him, feeling his love. If she had to choose a moment to stay in forever, this would be it.

"I'm so sorry you're stuck here alone," she said. "Knowing what is happening has to be worse than what I'm going through. How much time do we have before I leave again?"

"I think you broke the cycle. You have never remembered the actual attacks before now. I don't think you're going anywhere ever again."

"So now what? We walk into a bright light and disappear?" Maura held him tighter. She didn't want to let him go.

"I honestly don't know what we are now. I don't know what this place is—heaven, the fairy realm, a magic bubble, purgatory—but it's ours. We can have the life that was robbed from us for an eternity." Jack sprinkled kisses over her face.

"I can't believe you've been dealing with this for

thirty years. How are you not insane? To give up your life for," she gestured at the trees, "for this."

"I would wait a thousand years for just one more moment with you, Maura. Besides, you're a smart woman. I knew you'd find the truth eventually."

"How do you find something that you don't know you're looking for?" She ran her fingertip over the scar.

"By never giving up." He swept her up into his arms and began to carry her through the snowy trees. "I think the worst part was when you would come back and I couldn't say everything that was in my heart. How do you tell the woman you love, 'I love you', without being able to say it?"

"Everlastingly yours," she whispered into his neck.

"Yes. Everlastingly," he answered just as tenderly. "I don't know what happens now, my love, but we're together and that's all that matters."

The End

New York Times & USA TODAY
Bestselling Author

Michelle loves to travel and try new things, whether it's a paranormal investigation of an old Vaudeville Theatre or climbing Mayan temples in Belize. She believes life is an adventure fueled by copious amounts of coffee.

Newly relocated to the American South, Michelle is involved in various film and documentary projects with her talented director husband. She is mom to a fantastic artist. And she's managed by a dog and cat who make sure she's meeting her deadlines.

For the most part she can be found wearing pajama pants and working in her office. There may or may not be dancing. It's all part of the creative process.

**Come say hello! Michelle loves talking
with readers on social media!**

www.MichellePillow.com

facebook.com/AuthorMichellePillow

twitter.com/michellepillow

instagram.com/michellempillow

bookbub.com/authors/michelle-m-pillow

goodreads.com/Michelle_Pillow

amazon.com/author/michellepillow

youtube.com/michellepillow

pinterest.com/michellepillow

Warlocks MacGregor® Book 1
Contemporary Paranormal Scottish Warlocks

A little magickal mischief never hurt anyone...

Erik MacGregor, from a clan of ancient Scottish warlocks, isn't looking for love. After centuries, it's not even a consideration...until he moves in next door to Lydia Barratt. It's clear that the shy beauty wants nothing to do with him, but he's drawn to her nonetheless and determined to win her over.

Lydia Barratt just wants to be left alone to grow flowers and make lotions in her old Victorian house. The last thing she needs is a demanding Scottish man meddling in her private life. Just because he's gorgeous and totally rocks a kilt doesn't mean she's going to fall for his seductive manner.

But Erik won't give up and just as Lydia let's her guard down, his sister decides to get involved. Her little love potion prank goes terribly wrong, making Lydia the target of his sudden embarrassingly obsessive behavior. They'll have to find a way to pull Erik out of the spell fast when it becomes clear that Lydia has more than a lovesick warlock to worry about. Evil lurks within the shadows and it plans to use Lydia, alive or dead, to take out Erik and his clan for good.

Love Potions Excerpt

"Ly-di-ah! I sit beneath your window, laaaass, singing 'cause I loooove your a—"""

"For the love of St. Francis of Assisi, someone call a vet. There is an injured animal screaming in pain outside," Charlotte interrupted the flow of music in ill-humor.

Lydia lifted her forehead from the kitchen table. Her windows and doors were all locked, and yet

Erik's endlessly verbose singing penetrated the barrier of glass and wood with ease.

Charlotte held her head and blinked heavily. Her red-rimmed eyes were filled with the all too poignant look of a hangover. She took a seat at the table and laid her head down. Her moan sounded something like, "I'm never moving again."

"You need fluids," Lydia prescribed, getting up to pour unsweetened herbal tea from the pitcher in the fridge. She'd mixed it especially for her friend. It was Gramma Annabelle's hangover recipe of willow bark, peppermint, carrot, and ginger. The old lady always had a fresh supply of it in the house while she was alive. Apparently, being a natural witch also meant in partaking in natural liquors. Annabelle had kept a steady supply of moonshine stashed in the basement. If the concert didn't stop soon she might try to find an old bottle.

"*Ly-di-ah!*"

"Omigod. Kill me," Charlotte moaned. "No. Kill him. Then kill me."

"*Ly-di-ah!*"

Erik had been singing for over an hour. At first, he'd tried to come inside. She'd not invited him and the barrier spell sent him sprawling back into the yard. He didn't seem to mind as he found a seat on some landscaping timbers and began his serenade. The last time she'd asked him to be quiet, he'd gotten louder and overly enthusiastic. In fact, she'd been too scared to pull back the curtains for a clearer look, but she was pretty sure he'd been dancing on her lawn, shaking his kilt.

"Omigod," Charlotte muttered, pushing up and angrily going to a window. Then grimacing, she said, "Is he wearing a tux jacket with his kilt?"

"Don't let him see you," Lydia cried out in a panic. It was too late. The song began with renewed force.

"He's..." Charlotte frowned. "I think it's dancing."

Since the damage was done, Lydia joined Charlotte at the window. Erik grinned. He lifted his arms to the side and kicked his legs, bouncing around the yard like a kid on too much sugar. "Maybe it's a traditional Scottish dance?"

Both women tilted their heads in unison as his kilt kicked up to show his perfectly formed ass.

"He's not wearing..." Charlotte began.

"I know. He doesn't," Lydia answered. Damn, the man had a fine body. Too bad Malina's trick had turned him insane.

Warlocks MacGregor Series

Love Potions
Spellbound
Stirring Up Trouble
Cauldrons and Confessions
Spirits and Spells

More Books Coming Soon

to think of the man who saved her life, but she can't wrench her thoughts away. His words are those of a tyrant, true to his vicious reputation, but his touch is that of a man, stirring passion and lust when there should only be fear. It would seem the infamous monster is not as monstrous as he appears.

To learn more about Michelle's books visit:
www.MichellePillow.com

Chapter One Excerpt

Lakeshire Castle, Wessex, 879 AD

"God's bones, Ulric. Methinks this land of Wessex is making you soft!"

Vladamir of Kessen, the Duke of Lakeshire's voice was hard due to his exasperation. He knew his tone had a gravelly quality, which reflected a Baltic culture far to the northeast of the Saxon manor of Lakeshire. The heritage gave his softened words a hard bite as the harsh press of his lips gave his features a merciless appearance. Vladamir did it on purpose.

"'Tis irrational, foolish old man, for you to insist I stand downwind of that rotting pile of animal carcasses for nary an instant more. I don't know why you thought I'd be interested!"

His accent frightened the people under his rule. In fact, everything about him scared these people. He wanted the Saxons afraid of him. If they were afraid, they would follow his orders and leave him alone. He'd been in Wessex for a year and the plan had worked so far. It wasn't like he'd been sent to make friends.

Vladamir was the very first Duke of Lakeshire. It was a position he didn't relish. If he had his say, he'd live out his miserable days alone in a castle far away from everyone and everything. Either that or he'd gladly ride into another war.

Frowning sternly, he narrowed his eyes in annoyance and made no move to leave for his training exercises, though his fingers itched to grip his sword. Instead, he swept the fur lining of his cloak off his shoulder. The breeze lifted the weight of his unfashionably long, straight black hair off his shoulders and he absently watched the strands trailing away from him. He purposely wore the heathenish attire of those who lived in the Danelaw rather than to adapt to the more *civilized* dress of the nation of Wessex. He did it to irritate the Christian sensibilities of his Saxon neighbors and to drive fear into those men who were made to unwillingly serve under his rule.

Yea, everything about me is different than this accursed land. I'm a man without a country. I hate Wessex and I hate the land of my father. And I hate the peace between them both.

Tense, Vladamir raised his arm, motioning to the guard who stood above him on the dark stone of the bailey wall. A black onyx ring glinted on his finger, shining like a beacon the guard would be able to see. With a deft flick of his wrist, the duke silently commanded the knight to raise the outer gate.

The young, fair-haired Saxon didn't hesitate to follow his barbaric lord's order. Like all his subjects, Vladamir knew the guard watched him intensely for any sign of movement, no matter how small. It wasn't out of respect for him that the man instantly obeyed. It was out of fear. Fear was the reason all the Saxon warriors residing at Lakeshire Castle followed his command. They'd all heard the sinister rumors that followed him from his homeland, and he'd never tried to earn their respect or change their opinion of him.

Angrily, he jerked his arm, letting his irritation show. Vladamir knew what he was, knew what he looked like, and it was his intent to appear monstrous in both mannerisms and appearance. His linen undertunic was dyed to the pitchest of blacks. Although the material was of obviously rich quality, it lacked the perfected embellishments that frivolous nobles prided themselves on.

The sleeves of his tunic hung over his wrists and settled over the backs of his hands in long rolls. The undertunic fell loosely over his tightly fitted black braes, the long slit down the side showing a hint of his thighs. He fastened the material of the braes into place with laces that joined at the side and wore a plain, thick leather belt over them. From this belt hung an imposingly sharp knife and a modest leather pouch, which contained small pieces of flint for starting a fire and an iron key that fit a door the servants didn't even know existed.

"Clear it away at once. Methinks you have interrupted my morning training for naught more than fetid garbage." The duke ordered Ulric, only to growl in anger when the gate didn't rise fast enough to suit his impatience. He rested his hand on the hilt of his sword in warning. The action wasn't missed. Another knight disappeared off the wall, obviously going to hurry the man lifting the gate. Vladamir relished his ill humor, wallowing in it. "Argh!"

He sighed as the gate finally squeaked on its iron hinges, making the slow trip up. Gripping his sword, his scowl deepened. Instead of watching the gate, he stared at the hilt. The monstrous broadsword at his waist was in a leather scabbard, hanging from a leather shoulder baldric. The strap crossed over his chest so he could easily draw the weapon at the slightest provocation.

Still irritated, he glanced back to Ulric as the man tried to get a good view of the rotting animals through the gate's crosshatching. The servant turned to the duke, eyeing the nobleman's attire. Vladamir glanced down at his clothes, again thinking of how different he was from the Saxon men.

Over his tunic he wore a woven cloth belt of black and silver. It wrapped about his waist and knotted on the front right. He left the unadorned ends to drape freely about his thighs. The undertunic's oval neckline was laced high and tight against his thick neck, hiding the entirety of his chest from view. It was only on the rarest of political occasions that Vladamir was obligated to don an overtunic. He didn't feel the need of such formalities in his life when it came to dress. But, on those rare occasions, the overtunic was also black with very little silver embroidery.

The only relief to the investigating eye that Vladamir allowed was the lighter colored *rocc*, his fur cloak that was constructed of the skinned hide of several gray wolves. He would've dyed the fur black as well, if not for the ample waste of time and resources the project would consume. He wore the fur side inward for warmth as was customary among his fellow pagans.

"By all that is hallowed!" Vladamir growled, not caring who heard his cry. Many of the servants milling about the yard skidded to a stop at the sound. A small smile of devious pleasure automatically curled the sides of his mouth. It took a few seconds, but soon the servants were hurrying away in relief when they realized they weren't the cause of his present anger.

It was a well-known and accepted fact to the people of Lakeshire Castle that Vladamir had converted to Christianity solely to please King Alfred of Wessex in accordance with the Treaty of Wedmore. The duke did nothing to dissuade their beliefs or make them think that he was sincere in his conversion. Let them believe he was a devilish monster sent by King Guthrum to torment them.

In truth, Vladamir didn't much care for the Christian God, nor had he cared for the many gods of his ancestors. He lost faith when his wife died six years before. As he thought of it, it was quite possible he'd lost his faith before then.

Lowering his chin to glower down from his towering height, he curled his nose in disgust as another gust of wind assaulted him. The air carried a stench so severe that, even with his war-hardened training, Vladamir couldn't ignore the putrid smell. His expression turned quickly into a snarl. For all his rough appearance, Vladamir was a clean person, having been influenced by the peculiar bathing rituals of his father's people, the Vikings. He even insisted his household followed suit and bathed at least twice a sennight. It was a completely pagan routine little heard of in the dwellings of the Saxons. He'd received some protest over the decree, but it was necessary to keep such smells as these rotted animals out of his home.

His forehead wrinkled in irritation and tried unsuccessfully to determine what exactly emitted the foul odor. "What is it, Ulric? It smells of decaying flesh. Who would dare to lay carcasses afore my gate to rot?"

"Mayhap, 'tis a sacrifice in honor of the castle," Ulric offered with a grave shake of his head. The manservant's expression said he highly doubted it.

Ulric had traveled with the duke to Wessex the year before. A short man with a balding head, he had a pleasing face hidden under his trim beard. His jaunty nature was a direct contrast to that of his dark, forbidding lord—just as his rounded frame was opposite Vladamir's sinewy one. He wasn't only the duke's seneschal but was also the closest thing Vladamir could call friend.

"Nay, 'tis not the season for sacrifice," Vladamir answered as he looked up to the changing sky. It was early morning, yet the sky darkened to purple. He pulled the broadsword from his waist in one smooth motion and flexed the muscles of his sword arm in distraction, scuffing the tip across the dirt in a lazy stroke. Smirking, he said, "Besides, the prelate has forbidden such practices. 'Tis too barbaric a custom according to the church."

He sighed, fisting his hands as he pressed his lips tightly together. Upon closer examination, he discovered that the rotting bundle was actually an oddly shaped mound of pelts. Resting his fingers firmly upon his hips, he was mindful of the tip of the broadsword that still rested on the ground.

The stronghold's gate stopped above him, but he didn't bother to move. The gate was constructed of thick English oak and bound together with iron strips. The pointed ends at the bottom of the gate were wood reinforced with iron, causing them to act like metal teeth if lowered too quickly. Eyeing the spikes, he morbidly thought of how effectively they could sever a man in two.

Ulric rushed forward to the pile as soon as the spikes were out of his way. The seneschal's wider frame lumbered with the effort it took him to kneel and he grunted under the strain. Swiping the sleeve of his brown tunic across his forehead, Ulric placed his arm before his nose as he leaned closer to the pelts.

Impatient, Vladamir watched Ulric pick through the skins. He followed silently behind, refusing to sheath his sword. The seneschal sat straight up in surprise.

"M'lord, it would appear to be a maiden amongst these pelts. Methinks I see the entrails of a rabbit in her hair," Ulric yelled through the sleeve of his tunic.

The servant again wiped his sleeve across his

brow before returning it to his nose. His small brown eyes shone with concern. With a grumble of disdain, Ulric lifted entrails from the maiden's hair and flung them aside, only to gingerly remove a rabbit carcass the same way to reveal the bloodied lines of her swollen face. It was impossible to see whether she breathed.

In the distance, the sounds of fighting men and clashing swords filled the air as the knights competed in mock battle. A flock of wild birds flew high above to seek shelter from the changing sky. Their song softly drifted downward. None of the sounds pleased the duke as his eyes stayed trained on Ulric.

"A maiden? Out here? And scented with festering carcasses?" Vladamir searched the forest that surrounded his castle. The hum of insects was quite clear on the morning air, and he noticed that the red bristled pigs grazing just beyond his walls were undisturbed. Nor could he detect movement within the barren limbs of the trees. Finally satisfied that the girl was alone, he turned his attention back to Ulric. He refused to show any interest in the maiden.

"Wake her and send her on her way." He kept his voice passionless and made no effort to help the woman. "If she is dead, burn her, for I won't tolerate that wretched smell in my bailey."

"Should we not try to find out who she is first? Mayhap there are those who search fer her even now. Would you deny her kinsmen a proper burial?" Ulric protested quietly.

"Do as I command!" Vladamir insisted in a low growl. Even as he did so, he saw the knights that manned the wall look over the girl with curious stares. He heard their whispering as it drifted down, though he couldn't make out their hasty words. He didn't need to. The woman was more than likely a Saxon wench and they would wish to know whom, for none in the manor were missing. If she was dead, there was nothing he could do for her. He didn't need this headache. His life was stressed enough.

Through his irritation, Vladamir saw hesitation on the older man's face and quieted his tone to a logical murmur. "Is she dead?"

"I know not, m'lord." Ulric leaned to touch the girl and then turned back to his lordship. "She is not responding."

Vladamir tried to control his exasperation and repeated his original command, intentionally raising his voice to quiet the knights on the wall. His harsh accent made his words all the more lethal as he ground out, "Then she is dead. Burn her. I won't have her corpse carrying disease to the manor."

Ulric looked to him, searching the duke's face for a sign of compassion. Vladamir didn't give him one, refusing to be stirred to pity. It was easier to be feared than loved. It was easier to be dead inside than to feel.

Sighing heavily, the servant crouched over the girl. The duke stepped to the side, getting a better look at her. She was young and it was clear she'd been beaten. Her clothes were torn and her hair was matted with dirt and possibly blood.

Ulric yelled over his shoulder, loud enough to make sure the watching knights also heard his reply, "Nay, methinks she takes breath. She is not dead, merely insensible."

The duke frowned, knowing the servant hoped he wouldn't dare to leave a Saxon girl for dead, especially with so many soldiers to bear witness. If it had been a decade earlier, Vladamir would've carried the injured maiden into the castle to care for her. He'd have tended to her wounds, oversaw the physicians, stayed by her side until she was better. But the time was now and the duke would never allow himself to care like that again. Life had taught him some hard lessons.

Rubbing his brow, he then ran his fingers through the long locks of his tangled hair to brush it from his eyes. He shifted his weight from one leg to the other and didn't answer the servant. Scowling, he willed the maiden to disappear. He didn't want her in his home.

"Would you like me to leave her afore yer gate to rot? Or would you like to bring her in?" Ulric stood up and boldly matched his lord's stare, his thick jowls quivering in irritation.

Vladamir didn't like his servant's impudent tone and the man's sarcasm didn't go unobserved. He gritted his teeth as he asked with a sullen glimmer of hope, "Is she near death?"

"I know not." The servant once again turned from his overlord back to the pitiful girl. Thunder stuck in the horizon, beating its violent rhythm across the purple sky. The man pulled another carcass from her and tossed it aside.

"Check her." Vladamir purposefully sounded bored as he sheathed his sword. Anger was the easiest of all emotions and he clung to it. His gut tightened and he raised his eyes briefly to the heavens as a droplet of rain fell across his nose. "Be quick, Ulric."

Ulric felt the girl's pulse. "She has a good chance to recover if we move her indoors now."

Suspecting that the man might be lying, the duke paced in a frustrated circle, his hands fitted firmly at his waist. He rolled his neck until it cracked, debating the fate of the girl.

Those who moved about the bailey made their way toward shelter. A small page ran close to Vladamir, a pack of mongrel dogs quick on his heels. The boy laughed as a particularly ugly gray dog tripped him about the legs and sent him sprawling to the ground at the duke's feet. The page's face became wrought with fear as he looked up from the ground. The duke growled at him and the boy scurried away from him as the rain fell harder, hammering the ground with its loud music.

"It would appear she has been badly beaten," Ulric said. "Methinks it would be wise to move her inside, out of the rain, lest she is not like to live through the night. I can have a chamber readied for her abovestairs if you wish."

No matter how badly he wanted to give the order to leave her outside, Vladamir couldn't do it. He silently cursed himself for a fool and gave a self-depreciating laugh.

So much for being a complete monster.

"Yea," Vladamir conceded reluctantly. He stopped his pacing and turned to go, intent on leaving Ulric to tend to the woman.

"M'lord, wait." Ulric's urgent voice stopped him.

"Yea?" Vladamir gripped the hilt of his sword.

"M'lord, it would seem the maiden is a lady."

Please take a moment to share your thoughts by scrolling to the end of the document to rate/review this book.

Thank you for reading!

Be sure to check out Michelle's other titles at www.michellepillow.com

www.ingramcontent.com/pod-product-compliance
Lightning Source LLC
Chambersburg PA
CBHW030417120726
47904CB00007B/2308